Little Brother

Meagan E. Lambertson

ACKNOWLEDGMENTS

To Armoni

Nick had been only six years old when it all started and he'd thought himself the luckiest boy in the world. His parents sat him down at the kitchen table one night and he was sure he was in deep, deep trouble. Maybe more than the time he'd knocked over the vase and tried to hide it under the rug. But he couldn't for the life of him remember what he'd done wrong this time. Everything felt ominous as they sat down across from him, his mother sliding him a glass of chocolate milk. "Nick, baby," she'd said to him softly, a hint of a smile playing on her lips as she took his father's hand in her own. "Your daddy and I have decided that we want you to have a younger brother. How would you feel about that?"

Nick pursed his little lips as he thought about it. He supposed it could be fun, but weren't babies loud and messy?

His mother explained to him that this brother wouldn't be a baby and pulled up a picture on her phone to show him of a cute little boy with big eyes and big lips. "Nick," his mother told him, "this is Oliver. He has a mommy and a daddy that have made some bad choices. And Oliver needs a new place to live, and a new family to help him while his old mommy and daddy try to fix their mistakes. Do you think we could help him out?"

"How old is he?" Nick asked as though the answer would influence his decision, his eyebrows slightly furrowed.

"He's five years old," Nick's father chimed in. "And he could really use a smart, strong, older brother to show him how to be a good boy."

"Oh?" Nick studied the picture on his mother's phone carefully, zooming in and out to look over every detail of the boy's appearance. "I'm strong and smart." Nick said confidently after a few moments. "We should help him."

Matching smiles spread across Nick's parents lips and his father ruffled his hair. "That's my boy," he said with a soft chuckle.

Nick spent the next several days helping his mother get the house ready for Oliver. They cleaned out and organized the toys in his old playroom to make room for a bed. They went grocery shopping to make sure the fridge would be full for when Oliver got there. Nick was very worried the boy would be hungry. He looked so small in the picture he must be starving. While they were at the store, Nick picked out a stuffed shark for Oliver. All boys love sharks, Nick knew this because he loved sharks when he was five. This one was extra cool because it was a hammerhead. If Oliver didn't know about those, Nick could teach him.

Nick sat by the window nearly the whole morning on

the day Oliver was supposed to arrive, even though his mother told him Oliver wouldn't be there until after lunch. He was too excited to bother to do anything else. Even when his favorite show came on - the one about the animals in the wild - it wasn't enough to dampen Nick's anxiousness. At lunch time, his mother told him he couldn't go back to the window unless he ate a whole sandwich, so he scarfed it down before rushing back to his perch. By the time the silver car pulled into their driveway, Nick was watching through his toy telescope and sitting up high on the back of the couch, pretending to be the lookout guy on a ship. As soon as he saw the car pull in however, his little game of make believe was abandoned, telescope left on the window sill as he bounced around the living room yelling excitedly for his parents.

Nick hadn't thought much about having a younger brother before his parents had asked him, but in those three days before Oliver came, he'd thought about almost nothing else, imagining what Oliver would be like and how much fun they could have together. And in the year following, Oliver was everything Nick could have hoped for, and so, so much more.

Nick and Oliver watched television together, and they played games together. They made pillow forts and stayed up late in their forts on the weekends, eating popcorn and just talking. Sometimes Oliver would go away for a little bit. Nick's parents told him that Oliver was going to see his mommy and daddy. Whenever Oliver came back would have nightmares and wake up scared, and Nick sometimes helped him feel better. He tried so hard to be the best big brother he could be.

Nick loved Oliver even more than his shark collection and even more than his friends at school. When Oliver started going to the same school as him, they weren't in the same class, but Nick would sit with him on the bus and walk him to his locker. The pair never ran out of things to talk about or keep themselves entertained. Nick always easily found Oliver at lunch time and they would order different things and share their lunches. They would play together at recess, and Nick would meet Oliver at his locker at the end of the day again and they'd sit together on the bus ride home.

It was late in the afternoon on a Saturday when Nick's whole world came crashing down around him. Oliver had gone to stay with his parents for the weekend and Nick wasn't happy about it. He cherished every moment he got to spend with his younger brother and Oliver was usually quiet and upset when he came home after a whole weekend at his parents' house. Nick wanted Oliver to only be happy, so he'd dedicated his day to coloring pictures that he hoped would help make Oliver happy more quickly when he got back.

Nick was just finishing up a drawing of the two of them in their pillow fort with a plate of cookies. He signed it "Nicholas Michael. 7 years old. for Oliver my brother." And drew a big heart around the words before stacking it on top of the one he'd finished previously of the two of them swimming with a tiger shark.

"Nick, baby…" Nick's mothers' voice sounded shaky and he looked up to find her offering him a weak smile. "We need to talk."

Nick's head tilted in confusion as he put down the green crayon he was about to set to work with. "Talk about what?"

She held her hand out for him and Nick took it, getting to his feet. Once he was standing she scooped him up in her arms. Nick had gotten big. It wasn't often that his mother carried him anymore, but she carried him over to the couch and sat down next to his father, setting Nick in her lap. Nick shifted a little getting comfortable, and poked at the corner of his mother's frown. She drew in a shaky breath.

"Son," It was Nick's father that spoke and he turned to face him. "Oliver came to live with us because his parents weren't doing good things, and they got in trouble."

Nick nodded along. "Yes, and they couldn't take care of him, right? They make him sad." A choked sob slipped past his mother's lips and she gave a small nod, wiping at her cheeks. "Do they make you sad too, mommy?" Nick asked, redirecting his attention to her, a pout forming on his lips.

"Yes baby." She gave a small nod and sucked in a shaky breath, regaining her composure. "You did a great job, sweetheart." She gingerly brushed Nick's bangs back away from his face. "You were such a great big brother for him." A few tears slipped down her cheeks but her voice remained steady. "You helped him so much."

Nick's eyes flickered between his mother and father, unsure of where to even begin with the questions storming his brain. He watched quietly as his father rubbed soothingly at his mother's shoulders.

"Nick," Nick's father started again, taking the boy's smaller hand in his own and giving it a small squeeze. "Oliver's parents did everything they were supposed to do while they were trying to fix what they'd done. Now it's time for Oliver to go back and live with them again."

"What?" Nick's brows furrowed and his mother started rubbing his back soothingly like she did when he was sick or upset. "No. Oliver is my brother now. He can't go back."

"I'm sorry sweetie…" His mother's voice was barely above a whisper when she spoke. "Sometimes things don't work out the way we want them to."

"You don't understand!" Nick yelled squirming in her lap. She hugged him tightly to her chest and hushed him softly. "No, no!" He protested, squirming more. "Oliver is mine. I need him. He can't go."

Nick was never much of a crier. Usually when he got close to crying, he took a step back and thought about the situation. It wasn't something many children his age did, but he hated crying. It made him feel weak and childish, and Nicholas Michael was seven now. He was a big boy. Before he knew what was happening, a wave of emotion washed over him, accompanied by a wave of tears that he couldn't hold back. He fell limp in his mother's arms and sobbed into her neck until he fell asleep.

~~~

Nick wasn't off his game for very long. Sure, he thought about Oliver a lot after their last time together, and it made him sad, but he reminded himself that he was strong, and if he couldn't be strong, how could Oliver be strong?

Nick wrote Oliver a letter and drew a picture for him every weekend for a while and gave them to his mother to send. But he easily fell back in with his friends at lunch and recess. He continued watching his favorite shows, and sometimes his dad would hang out in his pillow fort with him. Everything was soon back to normal, as it had been a little over a year ago, before Nick even knew Oliver existed, although he still had a hard time watching the shark shows without Oliver. Now he preferred shows about alligators.

A few months later, near Nick's eighth birthday an unexpected guest arrived. Nick had woken at 8:30, the time he normally woke on weekends, and ate his cereal on the couch while watching his morning cartoons. He was a little suspicious when after
~~~

breakfast his mother forced him to take a bath so early in the day on a weekend. It wasn't unlikely for him to go out on a day as chilly as this one and play in his sandbox. He protested in earnest knowing she wouldn't let him go outside later if he'd already had his bath, but she insisted, and Nick was a good boy, so he did as he was asked.

His suspicion grew when she had him dress in his nice clothes. They weren't the super fancy ones like he'd had to wear to that wedding they'd gone to that one time, but they were like the ones she made him wear when his grandma wanted them to come to her church. Nick was more careful than usual as he ate his peanut butter sandwich for lunch, doing his best to not get it on his nice shirt.

After lunch he sprawled out on the couch with his father, half lying in the man's lap. His eyes were glued to the screen, the stuffed alligator he'd been holding forgotten as he watched the documentary on giant squids. Nick found himself completely infatuated with the creatures, hooked as soon as he learned of the size of their giant eyes. They could have very easily become his new favorite right then and there if his viewing hadn't been disrupted. Nick liked to make an educated decision. But he was just learning about the way the giant squid hunts its prey in the dark depths of the ocean when the screen went completely black. For a moment he thought they were just trying to emphasize the darkness that the giant squid lived in, but the sounds and the color didn't come back. "Daddy?" Nick asked in confusion.

"Hey bud." Nick's father, who had dozed off, smoothed down the young boys hair, mussed up from where he was laying on it. "We've got a guest, so be a good boy, okay?"

"Who is it?" Nick asked curiously, sitting up and peering out the window at the silver car that had pulled into the driveway.

"Honey," Nick's father called to his mother without answering him. "They're here."

Nick's mother rushed into the living room, tugging at Nick's clothing to straighten it out. She cupped his cheeks and smiled down at him. "Goodness, my little man is so handsome." Nick beamed proudly up at her, but before he could say anything, the doorbell rang and she jolted upright, rushing for the door. She paused in front of it for a brief moment, smoothing her fingers over her dress before pulling the door open. A beaming smile spread across her lips and her eyes flickered down. "Hello there." She cooed sweetly. Nick fidgeted impatiently next to his father, fingers curling into the fabric of his kaki's as he waited to see who was on the other side of the door. "Hi, come on in!"

As his mother stepped back out of the way a woman entered that Nick instantly recognized. She was the woman that had brought Oliver the first time he'd come to the house. His eyes flickered down to the scrawny boy at her side cuddling a little blue teddy bear to his chest. "Daddy?" Nick whispered excitedly, tugging at his father's pant leg.

The male crouched down beside him with a soft smile and whispered. "Yes, Nick?"

"Is she bringing Oliver again?" Nick whispered back, eyes searching his father's features desperately for a yes.

The older man's smile faltered for a moment but returned so quickly Nick wasn't sure if his eyes were playing tricks on him. "No, son." Nick's father shifted around to sit cross legged on the ground, taking Nick's hands in his own. "Oliver went back to live with his mommy and daddy again, remember? It's important for him to be with his family." Nick's father glanced over to the small boy holding the bear and the boy ducked behind the woman's leg, hiding. "This is Aiden," Nick's father told him. "He's gonna stay with us for a little while, okay?" A pout formed on Nick's lips but his father spoke before he could protest, brushing his fingers through Nick's hair to calm him. "He needs our help," he whispered quietly enough that no one but Nick would be able to hear him, "just like Oliver needed our help. So be a good boy, hmm?"

"I-" Nick started but quickly snapped his mouth shut again. He was nothing if not a good boy. And he wouldn't let his parents down. Certainly not in front of the lady that had brought Oliver to him. He gave a small nod, leaning into the soft touch of his father's fingers still running through his hair soothingly.

"Good boy," his dad muttered before turning himself

around to face the boy still tucked behind the woman's leg. "Aiden?" he asked, tone soft and sweet.

The boy had big round eyes, much bigger than Oliver's had been. He reminded Nick a lot of that cartoon he'd watched not that long ago with the baby deer in it. Nick shifted to sit next to his father, giving Aiden a small wave and the best smile he could muster, "hello." Aiden buried his nose in the top of his stuffed bear's head, peeking up at Nick through his lashes, but gave a small timid wave back. "Is that your bear?" Nick asked curiously reaching behind himself to grab the stuffed animal that had fallen to the ground by the couch earlier while he was watching T.V. "I have an alligator." Nick showed him, setting it on the ground and scooting it towards Aiden. "Maybe they can be friends." Hesitantly Aiden stepped out from behind the woman's leg and inched closer, eyes glued to Nick. He set his bear down in front of the alligator carefully before sitting down behind it. He peered up at Nick expectantly and Nick scooted himself closer. "How old are you Aiden?" Nick asked.

Nick's father ruffled his hair as he got up from the floor and as Nick and Aiden played, Nick's parents and the woman that had first brought Oliver and now Aiden, shuffled off to the kitchen for a cup of tea and a conversation.

Nick and Aiden got on fairly well. Aiden was quiet. He didn't talk unless Nick asked him a direct question, but Nick was more than happy to carry the conversation. Later after the woman left, they all sat down to have dinner. That was the first time things with Aiden started to rub Nick the wrong way.

Nick had shown Aiden to the bathroom, and the proper way to wash up before dinner, scrubbing with soap all the way up to his elbows. He led the way back to the kitchen and climbed up onto his own chair as his mother pulled out the one across from him. "Sit here, Aiden honey," she said offering him a warm smile.

"No!" Nick burst out before Aiden had even made it to the chair.

The small boy shrunk in on himself, taking a half step back. "Nick," his mother said in her serious voice, "what has gotten into you?"

"I-" A frown pulled at Nick's features as he glanced between his parents, the chair, and Aiden. "That's Oliver's chair…" he muttered softly. They hadn't had any guests since Oliver left and Nick had been very adamant about preserving his memory. This wasn't something, however, that he'd shared with his parents. He'd stopped using Oliver's old room as a playroom, reserving everything so that the next time Oliver came back, it would be as though nothing had changed, and the boy would know that Nick had waited for him, that nothing was different, and that they could still be brothers. But now Aiden was here.

Nick's mother let out a small sigh. "Baby, Oliver's not here. Don't you think Aiden could sit here? Shouldn't we all have dinner together?"

Nick's eyes flickered around the room. There really was nowhere else for him to sit. The table sat four, and that had always been plenty. Nick had never before thought his house was too small, but now it was starting to feel suffocating. He sucked in a deep breath, eyes landing on Aiden, nose again buried in his teddy bear and then turned back to his mother. "Yes. Aiden should eat with us."

"Come on up here, sweetheart." Nick's mother waved Aiden over. "It's okay." She lifted the five year old up onto the seat and scooted him in close before serving them dinner.

After dinner, Nick led Aiden back to the bathroom with his father close behind the pair. Nick's father leaned against the door frame, a fond smile on his lips as he watched his son pull open the top left drawer of the sink. "We keep lots of extra toothbrushes in here in case we have guests." Nick explained, fishing through the toothbrushes. "And toothpaste too. What's your favorite color Aiden?"

"I like red," Aiden muttered quietly, peering into the drawer.

Nick pulled out a red toothbrush, opened the box, and handed it over to the younger boy, flashing him a smile. "Here ya go." Nick glanced between Aiden and the sink, biting his lip. "Hang on!" Nick slipped past his father into the hallway and pulled open the closet there, grabbing out a small step stool he used to use when he was younger. "Excuse me," he grinned up at his father, and the man side stepped out of the way, ruffling Nick's hair as the boy passed. Nick set the stool down in front of the sink and gestured towards it. "Here, Aiden, you can use this. I used to use it when I was your age."

After a moment of hesitation, Aiden handed his teddy to Nick's father and climbed up the step stool. He teetered a little but Nick steadied him and stood close, offering support. Aiden grabbed ahold of Nick's shirt sleeve securely, holding his toothbrush in the other hand. A big smile spread over Nick's lips. He loved getting to be a strong, smart older brother. He grabbed the toothpaste and opened it, squirting some onto Aiden's toothbrush for him. "You should use as much toothpaste as uh… the same size as a pea." Nick told him. "Like this."

Aiden gave a small nod, still holding tightly to Nick's sleeve and watching as the older boy grabbed his own toothbrush from the holder on the counter, put the same amount of toothpaste on his own, and turned on the water, quickly swiping his toothbrush under it. Aiden copied his actions and soon Nick was singing his ABC's through a mouth full of foam and Aiden was swaying just a little, dancing along with the singing, a smile pulling at his lips. "You should always sing the ABC's when you brush your teeth." Nick told the younger boy as he dropped his toothbrush back into the holder. "Then you'll know you brushed them long enough." Aiden gave a small nod. "You can put your toothbrush here." Nick told Aiden, pointing to one of two still open spots. Aiden tucked it in next to the blue one that still hung where Oliver had left it the last time he'd used it. "Good job, Aiden." Nick praised the younger as he climbed down off the step stool, not letting go of Nick's shirt until he had both feet firmly planted on the ground.

By the time they finished brushing their teeth Nick's mother had joined his father in the bathroom door frame. "Alright boys," she flashed the pair of them a fond smile. "Time for pajama's. You have time for one story before bed."

"Can we read the alligator one?" Nick asked, bouncing excitedly down the hall towards his room. "I bet Aiden would like that one." Aiden took his teddy bear back from Nick's father and cuddled it tightly to his chest, bouncing along down the hall right behind the older boy, giggling a little.

"Sure son," Nick's father agreed, fingers curling around the handle of the door to Oliver's room. "Get your jammies on then bring the book down here."

Nick spun around as his father pushed the door open, eyes going wide. "No, wait!" He yelled in panic. Aiden shied away from the outburst burying his whole face in the top of his teddy bear's head as Nick rushed past him, blocking the door way.

"Nick…" his father's tone was full of concern and desperation. "Aiden is going to sleep in this room."

"No" Nick didn't often resort to whining, but it was clear now that he had no choice and he let it marinate his tone, "he can't."

"Baby..." Nick's mother crouched down, reaching for his hand but Nick pulled it away quickly, tears forming in his eyes before he could stop them.

"No. No, no, no. This is Oliver's room. This is his bed-" Nick's voice shook as he turned back to gesture into the room at the bed and tears streamed down his cheeks. "Those are his sharks, and his books, and his blankets. He needs them mommy, *please*." Nick wiped at his cheeks, a few choked sobs slipping past his lips as he tried desperately to explain the importance of the situation.

"Shh, baby," Nick's mother pulled him into her arms, hugging him to her chest and rubbing at his back in attempts to calm him. "Shhh, it's okay Nick."

"No, it's *not*." He insisted. "These are Oliver's and we need to leave them for him. Mommy, he *can't*- NO!" Nick's protests turned to a panicked screeching when his mother scooped him up and started carrying him to his own room. "No!" He squirmed in her arms, full on sobbing now. She nearly dropped him but managed to make it all the way to his room, kicking the door shut behind her and set him on the edge of his bed. "Mommy, p-pl-pleaaase" Nick begged, please don't let him sleep in Oliver's bed."

"Baby..." Nick's mother sat down next to him and he curled into her sobbing hysterically.

"Please, please no..." he continued muttering between sobs until he fell asleep.

The next morning, Nick woke feeling groggy. His throat was sore and his eyes felt puffy. He crawled out of bed and snuck out into the hallway. He creeped past his parents room, peeking in to find them both still asleep, and to Oliver's room. He tiptoed inside, just staring at the boy sleeping in Oliver's bed for a few moments. It hurt Nick's heart more than he could explain to see someone who was practically a stranger sleeping there. That bed, that pillow, that blanket, they all belonged to Nick's little brother. He wondered what Oliver would think if he came back to see someone else sleeping here. Nick could only assume that Oliver would feel unwelcome and that he'd think they'd forgotten about him or replaced him with someone else. Nick couldn't let that happen.

"Aiden," Nick hissed at the boy. Aiden didn't stir. Nick crept up to the edge of the bed and poked at Aiden's shoulder. "Aiden," he said a little louder, but not loud enough for his parents to hear him. "You have to get up."

Aiden's eyelids fluttered open slowly. A small smile spread over his lips when he saw Nick and he gave the older boy a wave, his other arm tightening around his teddy bear. It reminded Nick a little of the way he used to wake Oliver up to get ready for school or to watch cartoon's on a Saturday. It left a bad taste in Nick's mouth that he couldn't quite explain. It felt like he was replacing Oliver with this boy now.

"Get up, Aiden," he insisted, tugging at the blanket that the boy was tucked under. Aiden let out a soft groan, stretching much too slowly for Nick's liking and letting out a small yawn before rolling out of the bed. As soon as he was out, Nick started straightening the blankets, trying desperately to make it look like no one had been there, like it was freshly made, like it had been the last time Oliver had been in this room. There was a strange lump under the comforter and Nick reached in, fingers meeting something fuzzy and he pulled out a stuffed shark. He couldn't help the frown that colored his features when he saw it. Anger bubbled in his chest as he gave the stuffed shark a few small pets. He spun around to put it back on the shelf where it should have stayed, where Oliver had left it, and found Aiden standing there behind him. The small boy looked half asleep, eyelids droopy, hair mussed up, and a half smile on his lips as he watched Nick fix up the bed. "Get out." Nick practically growled the words at Aiden and pointed towards the door. "You're messing everything up. This is Oliver's room, not yours."

Aiden's smile melted away quickly and without a word he rushed out of the room into the hall and disappeared around the corner. Nick took his time carefully studying every inch of the room to make sure everything would be perfect for when Oliver came back. When he was done, he clicked the lock on the door handle and pulled the door shut as he made his way out into the hall so that no one would be able to get in until Oliver came back. He found Aiden there, sitting against the wall in the hallway starting to doze off.

"Aiden," Nick startled him awake again and the boy looked up at him with those large eyes wider than usual, lashes fluttering. "You can't go in there anymore." Nick told him pointing at the now locked door. That stuff isn't yours. It belongs to Oliver." Aiden said nothing, simply stared up at the older boy. "Oliver is my brother, got it? That's his room and his stuff and he's going to need it when he comes back so you can't-"

"Nicholas Michael!" It was his mother that had cut him off, in her serious voice again no doubt. "You get in your room right now!"

"But I-"

"No, now." Nick opened his mouth to protest again but the look on her face told him that he better not argue and he trudged off to his own room, grumbling about how important this was. "You stay in there until your father or I come get you, young man."

Nick had been stuck in his room for what felt like forever that day, and his parents were certainly not happy when they realized he'd locked the door to Oliver's bedroom. Things didn't get any better over the next few weeks either. Nick knew it wasn't Aiden's fault, he didn't even know who Oliver was, but he couldn't help the way he felt towards the smaller boy. Aiden was practically an imposter. Nick had watched a show before on stolen identities and he was sure that's what Aiden was doing. He was sleeping in Oliver's room, wearing some of his old clothes, playing with his toys, and reading his books. Aiden even got the same teacher Oliver used to have when he went to school with Nick. More than once Nick thought about calling the cops so he could make sure Oliver's identity was protected, but he'd been in enough trouble lately as it was, so he refrained.

The main thing that was different between Aiden and Oliver living in Nick's house was that Nick and Oliver always got along. But Nick and Aiden tended to fight. Aiden was usually quiet, but whenever Nick caught him playing with something that belonged to Oliver, he would take it away, and it always started with the two yelling at each other, progressed to wrestling over the toy, and ended with Nick alone in his room for a time out and Aiden getting to watch T.V. It was entirely unfair. As Aiden repeatedly got his way, he started to behave like the little brat Nick knew he was, sticking his tongue out at the older when his parents weren't looking and purposefully playing with Oliver's toys instead of the new ones Nick's parents had bought him.

Over the course of the month, they went to a few family events, one of which was Nick's birthday party. Nick had tried to be good all day long. For a few days there his mother had threatened to cancel the party because of his behavior and Aiden had been pushing all of Nick's buttons, but he bit his tongue and tried to ignore the younger. Despite all his best efforts, the joys of a birthday party didn't last nearly as long as they should have. Nick had been allowed to invite friends from school to the bowling alley where they were going to bowl, have pizza and cake, and play a few arcade games. Everything was going well, they'd played a few rounds of bowling and eaten the pizza and cake, and Nick had opened his gifts, but then it was time to go play laser tag. Nick's mother was urging Aiden to go join them, and one of Nick's friends asked who the little kid was. Nick's mother had said "This is Aiden, Nick's brother."

A scowl instantly colored Nick's features. "He's not my brother." Nick insisted. "Oliver is my brother." The angry glare he received from his mother didn't surprise Nick nearly as much as the shock and hurt on Aiden's face. The younger boy's shoulders slumped and he spun on his heel, trudging past Nick's mother, head hung low. Nick didn't have time to care, the game of laser tag was about to start. Aiden didn't join them.

The car ride home after the party was quiet and Nick got a good scolding about disrespect before bed that night. The next day was Saturday and when Nick woke in the morning, he found Aiden already up and sitting on the couch with a bowl of cereal. When Nick plopped himself down next to the boy, Aiden pushed the remote towards Nick without looking at him and scooted off the couch, making his way into the kitchen to eat at the table.

Things went smoothly for Nick for the next few days. His parents were still kind of mad at him for what he'd said at the bowling alley but he hadn't gotten himself into any extra trouble like he had been previously. It wasn't until the following Saturday, when Aiden left him alone on the couch again, that

Nick realized the boy hadn't so much as looked at him in over a week. Even though they fought a lot, Nick and Aiden still sometimes played together out in the sandbox, or they'd watch T.V. together after school. But Aiden had been completely avoiding him all week.

"Hey, Aiden?" Nick asked, following the boy into the kitchen. Aiden didn't answer. "Aiden, do you want to play outside with me?"

Aiden sat his bowl of cereal on the table and climbed up onto the chair, still not looking at Nick. "No."

"No?" Nick asked, tilting his head to the side. Aiden seemed to really like playing outside and it was going to be a nice warm day out, but not too hot. "And you don't wanna watch T.V.?" Nick asked.

"No." Aiden answered sharply, keeping his back to Nick and shoveling a bite of cereal into his mouth.

"Are you feeling sick?" Nick asked, shuffling closer and placing a hand on Aiden's forehead.

Aiden ducked away from the touch. "No." The boy scowled at him.

"Do you want to play sharks and ladders with me?" Nick asked, confusion pulling at his features at Aiden's reaction.

"I can't." Aiden said, turning back to his cereal.

"You can't?" Nick asked softly, but Aiden didn't answer, simply went back to eating. Nick huffed a frustrated breath and stomped back off to the couch grumbling to himself about Aiden ignoring him. He couldn't even get himself to enjoy his morning cartoons.

At lunch they ate together at the table like normal then Nick's mother loaded them up into the car and took them to the grocery store. Aiden got to sit in the cart his mother was pushing and Nick was following along behind, fingers brushing gently over nearly every packaged item they passed. They had just rounded the end of an aisle near the front of the store when Nick heard a familiar voice. "Later when we get home I can watch the show with the hammerhead shark?"

Nick's head snapped up as the bell chimed above the exit door and his eyes landed on a familiar mop of too long black hair. His muscles tensed up, as he watched the boy step over the threshold, practically bouncing in his excitement. He was taller now, and just as thin as he had been when he first came to live with Nick, but he had absolutely no doubt that it was Oliver walking away from him again. "Oliver!?" He called out, taking a hesitant step towards the door as it slid shut. The boy didn't seem to hear him. "Oliver!" Nick called again, taking off towards after him. He nearly crashed into the sliding glass door, bouncing in front of it as he waited impatiently for it to open, eyes glued to the young boy. Oliver locked eyes with him just as fingers curled into the fabric of Nick's jacket, holding him in place despite his efforts to get to his brother.

A beaming smile spread over Oliver's big lips and his eyes lit up when he spotted Nick.

Nick could see Oliver's lips form his name, and the boy waved frantically, but in the next second, his car door was shut and he disappeared behind the tinted windows. "Oliver…" Nick muttered before looking up at his mother who still had a tight hold on his jacket, tears welling in his eyes.

"I saw him, baby." She offered him a sympathetic smile and let go of his jacket in favor of brushing her fingers through his hair as he hugged her and buried his face in her stomach, drawing in a shaky breath.

Nick cried quietly the whole way home, and once they got there he headed off to his room to mope. Oliver had seemed happy. It sounded like he still got to watch the shark shows that Nick knew he loved. He'd smiled and waved cheerfully when he saw Nick. He didn't seem upset or like he was having nightmares, although he did seem really thin, but then, he was thin the entire time he'd lived with Nick despite Nick's best efforts to over feed him. The boy could eat a ton and still not gain weight. So Nick was less worried that he wasn't eating than he might have otherwise been.

Nick wasn't sure when he'd fallen asleep but he woke to someone sinking down onto his bed. He felt groggy again, like he did every time he woke up after crying. His mother and father were both sitting on the edge of his bed and he crawled over, climbing into his father's lap and burying his face in the man's chest, hugging him tightly. "How's my big boy?" Nick's father asked softly, fingers brushing soothingly over Nick's back. A soft whine slipped past Nick's lips as more tears threatened to spill out and he kept his face hidden. "Nick…" Nick's father let out a soft sigh and pulled back a little so he could look Nick in the eye. "You know you did so good for Oliver. You made him happy and you took such good care of him." Another whine slipped past Nick's lips as he listened and nodded along with his father's words. "You taught him so much and you helped him when his own family couldn't. You know that right, buddy?" Nick gave another small nod. "You helped Oliver get strong so that when he had to go back to his family he could take care of himself. Now Oliver is strong, just like his big brother Nick, right?"

"Yeah." Nick's voice shook and he wiped at the tears running down his cheeks. "He's strong and smart."

"That's right." Nick's mother flashed him a smile. "Because you taught him to be. But now, Oliver is back with him family, and he's happy and he's growing bigger and he's doing well. Don't you think Oliver looked like such a big boy now?"

"Yeah…" Nick muttered.

"Nick," Nick's father started again. "I know how much you love Oliver, and how much you miss him, but Oliver is okay with his family now. He loves them a whole lot. You remember how sometimes you go stay at grandma's house, and you love grandma and you have lots of fun there, but you always miss being home a lot?" Nick nodded. "Well coming here was kinda like that for Oliver. He loves you and he had lots of fun here, but he missed his home and his mommy and daddy. And now they can take care of him. They fixed their mistakes, and now Oliver can stay with them. Do you understand, son?" Nick looked between each of his parents, eyes glistening with new tears.

"Baby, you were such a good brother for Oliver, but he's not going to come back. He doesn't live here anymore. Sometimes, baby, you just have to let go. I know it's hard, we miss him too. But Oliver needs to stay with his mommy and daddy." Nick cried himself to sleep again that night.

The next morning, when Nick sat next to Aiden on the couch to watch cartoons, the younger still didn't talk to him, but he didn't get up and leave the room either. Later that afternoon, Nick found himself standing outside Aiden's room, peering in. He'd been avoiding it, knowing it would only make him angrier to see what they'd been changing. Now his eyes roamed the room slowly. The bed was messy, Aiden hadn't made it that morning, but everything else looked neat and organized. A new poster had been added to the wall of one of Aiden's favorite T.V. shows, but there was an entire shelf of shark toys and books that looked like it had remained untouched since the first morning after Aiden came to stay with them and Nick had put the stuffed shark back on the shelf. A soft noise had Nick turning around to find Aiden watching him.

Once Nick had noticed him, Aiden slipped past the older boy into the room and waved Nick in. He pointed towards the shelf Nick had been looking at. "I didn't touch these ones." He told the older. "You can take them if you want. Or they can stay here if you need them to." Aiden offered as he pushed himself up onto the edge of his bed.

Nick made his way slowly over to the shelf, eyes looking over each and every toy. Oliver had only been allowed to take one toy with him when he left, and he'd chosen the hammerhead shark Nick had given him on his first day there, even though he loved tiger sharks even more. Nick picked up the tiger shark from the shelf and cuddled it to his chest, burying his nose in it just like Aiden used to do with his teddy bear when he first came to stay with them. Even after all this time it smelled a little like Oliver. Nick inhaled a deep breath and when it came out again it was yet another sob. He hugged the stuffed shark tighter, flinching slightly as a pair of arms wrapped around his torso, but he leaned into the younger boy as Aiden rubbed at his back the way his mother usually did when he was upset.

About the Author:

Meagan Lambertson spends most of her days consuming an inhuman amount of caffeine and pretending to be a normal person in the real world. She is a master of procrastination and tends to golf so far above par it's almost unbelievable. Meagan holds an MBA and once lived in Taiwan, both as fruitless credentials here as they are in her day job. If you run into her at the store tell her no, she does NOT need another notebook.

You can find more from Meagan here: http://meaganlambertson.wixsite.com/authorsite

Note from the Author:

If you hate this, email me and let me know. meaganlambertson@gmail.com
Seriously.

www.ingramcontent.com/pod-product-compliance
Lightning Source LLC
Chambersburg PA
CBHW061410160726
47995CB00002B/545